2014

P9-DHM-765

Welcome to my BRILLIANT world....

Delia's
sunglasses

The Brilliant World of Tom Gates

By Liz Pichon

CANDLEWICK PRESS

First U.S. edition 2014

Library of Congress Catalog Card Number 2013952846
ISBN 978-0-7636-7472-4

14 15 16 17 18 19 BVG 10 9 8 7 6 5 4 3 2 1

Printed in Berryville, VA, U.S.A.

This book was typeset in Pichon.
The illustrations were done in mixed media.

Candlewick Press
99 Dover Street
Somerville, Massachusetts 02144

visit us at www.candlewick.com

Small
bug

Dedicated to **LOADS** of lovely people

♥ Mark ♥

Zak ♥ Ella ♥ Lily

Thanks to Sarah S.
And to my dad, who really
did wear some
Seriously
embarrassing outfits.

strong
bugs

Even though I only live four minutes away from my school, I'm often late.

This is usually because me and Derek (my best mate and next-door neighbor) "chat" a bit (OK, a LOT) on the way. Sometimes it's because we get distracted by delicious fruit chews and caramel wafers at the shop. Occasionally, it's because I've had loads of other very important things to do.

For instance, this is what I did this morning (my first day back at school).

Woke up — listened to music
Played my guitar
Rolled out of bed (slowly)
Looked for socks
Looked for clothes
Played some more guitar
Realized I hadn't done my "summer reading homework"

PANICKED — thought of good excuse for lack of homework (phew!).
Annoyed my sister, Delia. Which I admit did take up a very LARGE chunk of the morning (time well spent, though).
Hid Delia's sunglasses.
Took my comic into the bathroom to read (while Delia waited outside — Ha! Ha!). When Mom shouts ...

"TOM! You're LATE FOR SchooL!"

Run past Delia (who's still waiting outside the bathroom and quite cross now). Ignore her sisterly love.

CREEP!

Save precious time by:

Not brushing hair

Not brushing teeth (for very long)

Not kissing Mom good-bye
(Too old for all that kind of thing.)

Eat the last piece of toast, then grab my packed lunch and my bike. Shout BYE! to anyone who can hear me.

Then bike to school in about two minutes flat.

Which is a **New** TOM GATES WORLD RECORD.... And this is the REALLY good bit ... **AMY PORTER** has just arrived too!

 I am so pleased to see her after the holidays. I smile in what I think is a nice, friendly cheery way. 😊

Amy is not impressed. She looks at me like I'm weird (but I'm not).

Me smiling

HI, Amy!

(This is a bad start to my day.)

Then it gets worse....

Mr. Fullerman (my fifth year teacher) makes the whole class stand outside our room. He says,

"Welcome BACK, Class 5F. I've got a BIG surprise for you ALL."

(Which is not good news.)

OH, NO! He's rearranged ALL the desks! I'm now sitting right at the front of the class. Worse still, Marcus "Moany" Meldrew is next to me.

This is a DISASTER. How am I going to draw my pictures and read my comics? Sitting at the back of the class, I could avoid the teacher's glares. But I am SO close to Mr. Fullerman now I can see up his nose.

And if that's not bad enough, **M**arcus Meldrew IS the most annoying boy in the WHOLE school. He is SO nosy and thinks he knows everything.

Marcus Meldrew is already annoying me....

He is looking over my shoulder while I'm writing this.

He is **still** looking.... ⊙ ⊙

Still looking....

Yes, MARCUS, I'm writing about

⇒ YOU ⇐

MARCUS MeLdrew

has a face like a mouse.

Marcus Meldrew has a face like a

Moose!

Moosey Marcus . . .

(He's stopped looking now.)

Bu⊤ on the other side of me, the good ☺ news is I am now sitting next to 😊 **AMY PORTER**, who is very smart and nice (even though she didn't seem thrilled to see me this morning).

BrILLIANT! ⭐ At least I can have a sneaky look 👀 over her shoulder for a few right answers.

I think she is looking at me now.

AMY PORTER is <u>very</u> nice.

AMY PORTER is *SMART.*

☺

10

She's not looking.

She's ignoring me.... I think.

So I might as well stop writing nice things now and draw a doodle instead.

(This cheers me up.)

Marcus
gets squished by a

BiG
Monster

Then Mr. Fullerman says,

"As you can see, I've changed a few things around."

(Don't I know it!)

Then he begins to take attendance.

(Usually I would take this opportunity to draw a few cool pictures, or take out my comic for a quick read. But I'm SO close to Mr. Fullerman and his beady eyes ⊙ ⊙ that I have to wait until he finishes and walks to the back of the class before I can get doodling in my book.)

Ok, he's gone now. I'm thinking of names to call my band that Derek and I are in. We're not very good YET, but if I can think of a really good name, that will make us seem extra cool.

Ｈow about ALIEN TWINS? FOOT FIGHTERS?
I know ... DOGZOMBIES.

Mr. Fullerman interrupts my drawing (I've turned the page over fast so he can't see it) and hands out the first piece of work we have to do this term. (Groan.)

Vacation Story Writing

Welcome back, Class 5F.

Today I would like you to write a story about what you did on your summer holidays.

* Did you go away?
* Did you visit your family?
* What was the weather like and where did you stay?

Remember to describe everything in detail.

I am really looking forward to reading all about your vacations!

Mr. Fullerman

My summer wasn't a great success,
but it does have a very happy ending....
Here goes ⇨

Camping Sucks

This year, Dad said, "Let's go camping, it's cheap." Mom didn't seem that keen, but I'd never been camping before, so I was looking forward to it.

Dad and I went to the camping shop to buy a few essential items like:

"We won't need much," he said.

Dad

1. Tent
2. Sleeping bags
3. Cooking stuff
4. Fishing rods
5. ~~TV~~
6. ~~Computer~~

But the camping shop had some cool stuff, and Dad got carried away. He spent a LOT of money and made me promise not to tell Mom.

"We could have stayed in a nice hotel; it would have been cheaper," Dad said.

"Not the same as sleeping under the stars and waking up in the fresh air!" said the man in the shop as he took Dad's money.

On top of everything Dad bought, Mom packed a whole lot more. The car was stuffed. My sister, Delia, wasn't happy about coming with us.  She's not allowed to stay in the house on her own anymore, because she had a **WILD** party the last time Mom and Dad went away. (I stayed next door with Derek. His parents got woken up and weren't happy either.)

We set off, and for a while the trip was going well. Then we took a wrong turn and got lost.

Mom blamed Dad for not listening to her properly. Dad blamed Mom for not reading the map the right way. They both blamed each other.

It was only when the car got a flat tire that they stopped arguing. They phoned the Car Rescue Service, who eventually turned up.

It took AGES to fix the tire, and we didn't make it to the campsite until it was dark. Delia wasn't happy. (Delia's never happy.) She said the place looked RANK and plus she couldn't get a signal for her phone. Ha! Ha! Ha! I thought it looked OK. So I helped Dad with the tent while Mom unpacked the car. (Delia did nothing.)

The tent was tricky to put up, but we did the best we could.

It was a bit late to eat. Dad said, "I'll cook a big breakfast in the morning." But my stomach kept **rumbling** and I couldn't get to sleep. Then I remembered the secret stash of wafers in my bag. So I grabbed them and ate them all! Crumbs got everywhere and it was very uncomfortable in my sleeping bag. Even though we had a "family tent" with separate rooms, Delia could hear me shifting around and fidgeting. It was really annoying her. **BRILLIANT!** So I did it some more. But at the same time, I could also hear Mom and Dad ...

SNoring —and that

was keeping me awake too. The noise was awful.
It seemed to be getting louder and LOUDER.
It was almost like thunder, deep and rumbly.
Then I realized it sounded like thunder ...
because it was thunder. Which was getting
closer. There was lightning too, and
really heavy rain that was right
above our tent. The storm was
HUGE, and it didn't take long for
the tent to blow away. AGH! HELP!

Everyone had to run to the car for
cover. The storm lasted all night long, and
everything we had got wet and muddy.
Dad had pitched the tent RIGHT NEXT TO
A STREAM! It flooded and all our stuff got
soaked.

Nobody slept at all. It was miserable.

Spot the problem . . .

In the morning, Dad tried to get his money back from the campsite owner (while we slept in the car).

He complained a lot, but it didn't work. Mom collected our soggy belongings, which were all ruined (including the tent). I could hear her muttering things like "Proper vacation next year" and "Greece" under her breath.

Delia was crying (again) because her mobile phone had gotten wet and wasn't working. That cheered me up. So I decided to try and make the best of the holiday and go exploring. There were lots of interesting-looking trees to climb. I was nearly at the TOP of one when suddenly a branch SNAPPED under my foot.

I hadn't realized how high up I was until I fell down....

It was pretty impressive, really....

Delia heard me YELP as I hit the ground. She came over and just watched me as I rolled around on the ground in pain, holding my arm. It felt REALLY BAD but Delia didn't look too concerned.

Ha!
Ha!
Freak!

Eventually she got Mom.

24

"That's all I need," said Mom as she took me to the first-aid tent. They gave me a lollipop 🍭 and put my arm in a bandage (I was very brave). 😊

It looked like our camping holiday was going to be very short. More rain was due, so Mom and Dad decided that under the circumstances (no tent or dry clothes) we should go home. 🙁

I wasn't that upset, and Delia was delighted. So we all packed up and left the campsite. 🪧Home

On the way home we stopped off in a nice restaurant, where I managed to eat a huge pizza with my one good arm. My bad arm was really hurting 🙁 but I didn't complain because it was the first time in ages that everyone looked happy.

Our neighbors Mr. and Mrs. Fingle and Derek were surprised to see us back so soon. My bad arm was SO painful now that I went to my room to look at it.

Worryingly, it had turned purple and SWOLLEN up like a balloon.

I showed Mom and Dad. They looked shocked. Delia said, "You look like a FREAK" (which was kind of her). Mom and Dad got back in the car and drove me to the hospital, leaving Delia at home.

Luckily ... my arm's not serious. I had just sprained it, and the bandage was put on too tight. So they redid it and put it in a very cool sling instead.

(I'll live, apparently.)

It was quite late by the time we got home and there was music BLASTING out from our house. Mom and Dad were FURIOUS.

Delia had invited lots of her friends over for a party, and BOY was she in trouble.

I forgot all about my sore arm because listening to Delia being told off and grounded by Mom and Dad was probably the → BEST PART of my whole entire holiday.

What were you thinking?

You're grounded!

Yeah!

THE END

It sounds like you had a very
eventful time, Tom!
Excellent work. I felt like I was
there ... but glad I wasn't!

5 Merit Points

WOW! Mr. Fullerman liked my story!
I've never had **5** merits before.
I leave the page open so **AMY PORTER** can
see how clever I am. But she doesn't seem
too interested. Maybe this will help:

I got 5 MERITS

No, she's still not looking.

Marcus says he's got five merits as well.

"Great," I say.

"We're like twins now," says Marcus.

(He's so annoying.)

I show Mom and Dad my story because I think they'll be pleased with me (for a change).

Instead Mom gives me a note to give to Mr.
Fullerman.

Dear Mr. Fullerman,

We are delighted Tom got five merit points.

Also, can I just say that this is not the
usual type of vacation we have. We are
actually VERY responsible parents.

Tom's arm is fine now — in case you were
wondering (and in case he tries to get
out of doing P.E.).

Kind regards,
Mr. and Mrs. Gates

I think Mom was worried my story made them
look bad.

BREAK time!

I am catching up with a few friends who I haven't seen over the holidays. Mark Clump got another pet (but he won't tell me what it is!).

Norman Watson's not allowed to eat candy or ANYTHING with sugar in it because it makes him go really WILD. But I can see him running around the playground with his sweater over his head shouting, "I'm a spaceman, I'm a spaceman." Which makes me think he's had a few sneaky sweets already today.

Solomon Stewart (his nickname's SOLID) is the tallest boy in the whole school. He has GROWN even more, I think.

Then Derek comes over (he's in Mrs. Worthington's class, not mine, because we chat too much). I've seen him loads during the summer. (His hair has grown—he hasn't.)

I show him my ideas and drawings for a band name. (He likes DOGZOMBIES best ... me, too.)

When Marcus Meldrew barges into our chat....

"What's that?"

"Ideas for our band."
"What band?"
"Me and Derek are in a band, and we're thinking of what to call ourselves."
"That's easy."
"Really?" (Marcus has an idea.)

"**Y**eah.... Just call yourselves

'The Total Losers.'

Ha! Ha! Ha!" says Marcus ...

who's even more annoying this year than he was last year (if that's possible).

Marcus being a **TWIT**

Ha! Ha! Ha!

There's homework already from Mr. Fullerman. (It's like we never had a holiday.)

HOMEWORK

I'd like you all to write a REVIEW.

It could be a review of a book, play, concert, or film: something you have seen or read.

Ask yourself lots of questions:

Describe the film/book/concert.
What did you like or not like?
What was it about?

Looking forward to reading them very much.

Mr. Fullerman

(I'll see what's on TV tonight, then read the newspaper review. That's always a good start.)

Mr. Fullerman's
SHADOW

Sitting so close to Mr. Fullerman is already
proving tricky for me.
Because I am being forced to work.
It's EXHAUSTING!

(Amy doesn't seem thrilled to be sitting
next to me. Maybe if she sees me working,
she'll think I'm smart?
I will try to impress her.)

She's just caught me sneaking a look at her
work. I pretend to be drawing, but I've been
rumbled.

I know ... I'll draw something FUNNY.

Mr. Fullerman with hair ...

(Amy still not impressed.)

After class, I meet Derek by the bike shed.
Our bikes are very cool. Mine's covered in
stickers and doodles. Derek's is a bit battered
but *super* fast. There's a very odd-looking bike
in the shed that catches our eye (not) in a
good way).

It's covered in FUR and FLUFF
with silly wobbly eyes and weird bits
hanging from the handles.

"It looks like Marcus," Derek laughs.

"Or Norman Watson on candy!" I say.

"Bet it belongs to a little new kid who doesn't know any better!" says Derek.

"What kind of person would have a stupid-looking bike like that?" I laugh.

Ha! Ha! Ha! Ha! We both laugh!

Ha! Ha! Ha! Ha!

But **AMY PORTER** is NOT laughing because it's her bike.

School janitor Stan is shaking his head and tutting in a disapproving way (which is making his keys jangle) because I have upset Amy (AGAIN!). She calls me an **IDIOT** and takes her bike away. I say "Sorry," but Amy ignores me. (She ignored my five merits, too.)

TuT
TuT

It's been a terrible day.

On the way home, I see posters for my favorite band, **DUDE 3**, all over town.

Even this doesn't cheer me up.

Derek does his best to make me laugh.

But all I can think about is Amy calling me an idiot (harsh) and Marcus calling us losers.

"Look on the bright side," Derek says.

But when I ask Derek what the bright side actually is ... he doesn't know.

"It's a saying."

Great.

I'll have to think of a way to make it up to Amy, which is not going to be easy.

Band practice with Derek tonight might not be so good because there's absolutely NOTHING that will cheer me up now.

Not a thing....

MOM'S

BOUGHT

CARAMEL WAFERS

Caramel Wafers

FANTASTIC!

Brilliant! MY Favorite!

Hooray, Hooray, Hooray! Hooray!
Hooray, Hooray, Hooray! Hooray!
(I've suddenly cheered up.)

42

Derek and I eat two caramel wafers each and drink some orange soda. (Perfect preparation for band practice.)

Mom tells me to:

"Leave one for Delia!"

(As if!)

Instead, I take the last one and show Derek my favorite wafer trick.

Which goes like this:

1. Remove last caramel wafer  from wrapper really carefully.

2. Eat wafer quickly before Delia comes home (half each).

3. Carefully re-fold wrapper to look like wafer is still inside. (empty)

4. Watch Delia open the empty wafer wrapper (ha, ha).

My trick worked a TREAT.

I can hear Delia moaning to Mom about me downstairs. So I take the opportunity to sneak into her room and borrow a few copies of **ROCK WEEKLY** for Derek and me to look at.

(Good inspiration for band practice. There are loads of good pictures of bands inside.)

We take turns trying out a few

ROCK STAR POSES.

Delia's sunglasses

Some of them are more successful than others.

(Mustn't forget to do this week's homework —
write a review....Should be easy.)

Mr. Fullerman:

I'm very <u>SORRY</u>.

You'll never guess what happened.

I had just finished writing my homework review when I accidentally spilled the **BIGGEST** glass of water all over it.

I am very upset, as it was a **VERY** good review. (Probably worth at least five merit points, if not six.)

AGH!

Oh dear, Tom!

What a mess. I will look forward to seeing it redone for tomorrow. Watch out for those BIG pesky glasses of water in the future!

HomEwork

(I think I got away with that excuse, will
definitely write review for tomorrow.)

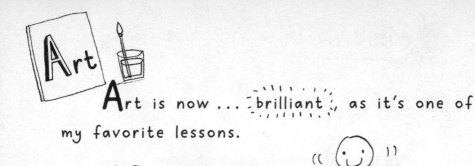

Art is now ... brilliant, as it's one of my favorite lessons.

Mr. Fullerman would like us all to draw a self-portrait.

These will be put up around the **WHOLE SCHOOL** for everyone to see (and laugh at, probably).

Mr. Fullerman hands out small mirrors so we can look at ourselves while we're drawing (which is not easy at all).

Everyone is concentrating and quiet for a change, apart from Norman Watson, who keeps shining his mirror in other people's faces, until he's moved.

Then Mrs. Worthington (Derek's teacher) comes in and takes over from Mr. Fullerman, who goes off to do something more important (like drink coffee and read newspapers).

Mrs. Worthington sometimes takes over for math. She is always very enthusiastic about everything. She is being very enthusiastic now.

Hello! Hello! Lovely Class 5F!

"I'm looking forward to seeing all your lovely pictures," she tells us happily.

Because I like art and drawing, I'm working extra hard.

Amy's self-portrait looks a bit odd. (She doesn't really look like that at all.)

Hers is still better than Marcus's. He's drawn himself with a really BIG head (well, that bit's true to life).

Mrs. Worthington sees I've finished my portrait and comes over to take a closer look.

"*What a marvelous picture, Tom!*" she says.

"*Mr. Fullerman will be pleased!*" she adds.

But I'm not really listening to her ... because I have suddenly noticed that this close up, Mrs. Worthington has something on her top lip that looks a bit like, well,

 like a ...

MUSTACHE!

I am trying really hard not to stare.
(It's tricky not to.)

(Don't stare.... Don't stare....
Look at her face, not her mustache.)

"Tom, why don't you do another
wonderful portrait?"

Good idea.

"Only this time, really think about
the person you're drawing. And don't forget to
put in *LOTS* of detail."

OK, Mrs. Worthington,
I'll do my best.

Here goes....

I'm getting the feeling that Mrs. Worthington
doesn't like my portrait (or me) very much
now.

Oakfield School
Re: Tom Gates

Dear Mr. and Mrs. Gates,

I'm very sorry to inform you that Tom has detention tomorrow at lunchtime. This is due to an unfortunate portrait he drew of me. I do hope Tom will learn the lesson that there is a BIG difference between drawing a portrait with detail ... and just being rude.

Yours sincerely,

Mrs. Worthington

(Lesson learned. Don't let teachers see my drawings in future.)

When I get home, Dad ALREADY knows about my detention because Mrs. Worthington has phoned. (☹) And more bad news—Delia took the phone call so she knows about it, too.

GREAT, like the letter wasn't enough. Mrs. Worthington might as well have announced my detention with a plane TOM has Detention! or a hot-air balloon TOM HAS DETENTION so everyone in the whole town knows. (Groan.)

Dad tells Mom, and now Derek isn't allowed to come over for band practice tonight. AND she's making me do an extra chore.

"Sweep the kitchen floor or take out the bins" (which smell). Some choice.

Delia is LOVING this. She keeps saying "Poor little Diddums" to me in a really stupid baby voice, which is driving me crazy. (But I can't let her see she is getting to me, or she'll keep on saying it ALL night long, and probably tomorrow and the next day, too.)

Dad gives me one of his little chats and tells me if I don't work hard at school, I'll end up like him. Not such a bad thing if you ask me, because Dad's got a pretty good job.

Chat Chat

He has his own office (well, it's a shed in our garden) where he works on his computer, designing stuff. Occasionally he gets to work in other people's offices.

Mom likes it when that happens because he has to dress up and he earns more money.

I prefer it when Dad works at home because he has a SECRET stash of caramel wafers Cookies in the shed that I eat (and Mom doesn't know about).

So there I am sweeping the kitchen floor when Granny Mavis pops over to borrow a cookbook.

Hello, Tom! Just popping by to pick up a cookbook!

(I call my granny and granddad

because they
are both old
and very ancient.)

"You never use cookbooks!" Mom says in a surprised way.

"I'm inviting the whole family round for lunch," Granny says.

"Really?"

(Oh, dear.... That's not really 😟 very good news. Let me explain. ...)

Granny Mavis and Granddad Bob are not your usual kind of grandparents.

Especially when it comes to meals. They like to experiment and eat very odd combinations of food.

pear   onion   soup

tea

cornflakes

(Saves time apparently.)

(More on that later.)

Also, Granny is just RUBBISH at cooking. So Mom loads her up with a pile of cookbooks in the hope that she might actually follow a real recipe.

I'm still sweeping and trying to make Granny feel sorry for me by doing my

"sad face." Hopefully she'll slip me a bit of extra pocket money (Granny does that sometimes).

But Mom tells Granny │why│ I'm sweeping the kitchen.

Oh, dear...

Rude drawing!

("Detention ... blah, blah ... drawing ... blah, blah ... mustache ... blah, blah.")

And *now* she wants me to go to the shop to buy Milk! (work, work, work) "So Granny can have a cup of tea."

Luckily Granny gives me extra money to buy myself a treat.

RESULT

In the shop, I'm deciding how to spend my treat money (sweets? caramel wafers?) when I spot ⊙ ⊙ this week's copy of

ROCK WEEKLY

And on the cover is the best band in the whole world,  DUDE 3.

I **HAVE** to buy it! And there's even enough money left over for two fruit chews.

  BRILLIANT!

Mom asks,  "Where's the milk?"

(Suddenly I remember why I went to the shop and hide my copy of **ROCK WEEKLY**.)

"The shop had run out," I say.

(*PHEW!* Quick thinking ... must tell Derek about **DUDE 3**.)

Granny Mavis has hot water with a slice of carrot instead, which is a bit bonkers even for her.

Odd

I have read the whole interview with **DUDE3**. And I can't believe they are actually coming to play a concert *IN* OUR TOWN.

I go on the computer to listen to their latest tracks and see where else they're playing.

This is AMAZING. Derek is online and is just as excited about it as I am.

 Dude3 Dude3 Dude3! WHOOOOOO HOOOOOOO!!

Can't wait, DUDE MAN. Will SO be there!!!

 ME TOO ... BRILLIANT!! Can I read your mag after? Bring to skool yeh!

Spread the DUDE3 word. Dad calling, time for burnt food.

 Pretend it's fast food ... and eat it really fast ... LOL!

Ha! Ha! Give it to Delia ... she won't see it with her dark glasses. FREAK!

Good news about the concert. **B**ad news—me and Derek are too young to go on our own. Dad will probably want to come, too. Which is OK as long as I can get him to **PROMISE** not to:

1. Sing

2. Dance

3. Wear anything embarrassing

Shame

Which could be tricky because he likes to do all those things (sometimes at the same time).

I did it MY way.

(Go back to reading my **ROCK WEEKLY**.)

Hardly slept at all last night. ☺, ☺

All I can think about is

coming to town. FANTASTIC.

Even Delia seems excited. (For her, anyway....
It's hard to tell.)

As long as she doesn't stand anywhere near
me, I don't mind.

The tickets cost a LOT of money.
If I'm going to get DAD to pay for them,
I will have to be on my best behavior at all
times. This will be tough but worth it.

I'm reading my copy of **ROCK WEEKLY** in the bathroom while Delia is ¡BANGING¡ on the door outside. The crosser she gets, the slower I read, and brushing my teeth takes AGES.

It makes me late for school again (worth it, though). So I don't bother brushing my hair and just grab my clothes off the floor to wear (they're crumpled ... but who cares).

clothes pile

Then I stuff as much toast in my mouth as possible and take an apple to eat on the way (which is not easy on a bike).

Toast

I make it to Mr. Fullerman's class with **30** seconds to spare.

Me being busy

I'm feeling pretty pleased with myself, so I try another cheery smile at Amy, who for some reason makes a "YOU'RE DISGUSTING" face at me.

Why?

Me Smiling

Hi, Amy!

Mr. Fullerman announces,

"I hope you've all remembered it's your Individual School Photo today."

NO! NO! NO!

(I forgot.)

Smug mug Marcus obviously did remember. He's looking all shiny neat and new. Ugh.

I'm looking slightly more crumpled than usual due to my rushed start to the day. Oh, well. Never mind. How bad can a school photo be?

The whole class lines up in the hall. I'm second in line after Norman Watson, who is all twitchy and jumpy. (I really hope Norman hasn't eaten any sweets.)

The photographer asks Norman to "stop jiggling around."

(Oh, dear.... He's definitely had some.)

Eventually (after LOADS more goes) Norman sits still just long enough for one photo to be taken.

The photographer whispers,

"This is going to be a very long day."

Then it's my turn.

Florence Mitchell  (another super-smart girl) and Amy are watching me along with the rest of the class.

I have an idea. I will try and look all MEAN and MOODY, a bit like the photos of DUDE3 in ROCK WEEKLY.

BRILLIANT!

But the photographer is not impressed and tells me to "CHEER UP!"

So I try and smile (a bit) ... then he says REALLY LOUDLY:

"Oh, dear. You've got something NASTY stuck between your teeth."

(SHAME!)

He walks over and hands me a mirror. (Could this be any more embarrassing?)

"Better do something with your messy hair, too—here's a comb."

Now EVERYONE is looking at me.

(It just got a lot more embarrassing.)

I have toast crumbs around my mouth and bits of apple skin stuck between my teeth. (Why didn't Amy <u>tell</u> me?) And now I've gone bright red, too.

So much for a cool school photo. It's going to be hideous. ☹

The photographer takes my picture and I can't get out of the hall fast enough. I have humiliated myself in front of the

ENTIRE class.

Now I will be forced to hide this school photo from everyone for the rest of my life, especially Mom. She likes to send my school photos to <u>all</u> relatives across the

WHOLE WIDE WORLD.

ToM'S School Photo

There are second cousins in Outer Mongolia who have my school photos on their walls.

To Vera Gates
5 Green Lane
Outer Mongolia
The World
(Tom GATES's photo enclosed)

BREAK TIME

I'm looking for **D**erek on the playground and I can't find him anywhere. His bike is in the shed, so I know he's here. I wonder if his school photo was as bad as mine? (Impossible.)

I ask Solomon "Solid" Stewart (the **TALLEST** boy in the whole

school) if he can see Derek.

VERY TALL

Solid points to a boy on the climbing frame. He looks a bit like Derek, but it can't be him because his top button is done up AND he's got a horrible, neat side part.

SIDE PART

"Mom made me," Derek says. "For the school photo." (Shame.)

Then Derek hangs upside down on the climbing frame and his hair goes back to normal. Which is just as well, because no one in

DOG ZOMBIES should ever have a neat side part like that.

More importantly, Derek and I chat about . . .

1. How  is the BEST band ever.

2. How we REALLY need to go and see them.

3. How  need to practice more to become the BEST band EVER.

4. COOKIES – which are better, chocolate or caramel wafers?

5. And which to eat at band practice.

chocolate   or   caramel?

Who cares about stupid school photos?

Wafer
Doodles

WAFER

WAFER

AGH!

MATH

Mr. Fullerman hands out our math worksheets.

On the outside I'm forcing myself to look fascinated and interested in Mr. Fullerman's sums 😊😐 —when really on the inside I am still reliving the humiliation that was my school photo, over and over and over again.

HIDEOUS School Photo

I wish it was the end of school right now. So to cheer myself up, I draw a few more band logos and ideas.

I'm careful to do some sums as well so it looks like I'm "working out" my answers.

A dog that's a zombie

Which one?

24 +
32
56

DOG
ZOMBIES

DOG
ZOMBIES

DOGZOMBIES

10 +
10
20
← I am a Genius!

Marcus is straining his head and trying to look over my shoulder so he can see 👀 what I'm doing.

GET LOST, MARCUS . . .

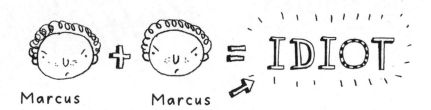

Marcus   +   Marcus   =   IDIOT

Mr. Fullerman is looking at me now. So I put my arm right over my drawings and do a few more sums.

Zombie marcus

Improvement!

$$10 \times 10 \over 100$$ Smart

DOG ZOMBIES

Marcus is LEANING back in his chair now to see over my arm. I think he can see my doodles, so I turn my back on him. And he leans *FORWARD*. Then I LEAN back, and he puts his head on the table as if he's trying to see under my arm. Ha!

"MARCUS ... stop trying to look at Tom's work and concentrate on your own!"

Yes, Marcus, NO cheating. Serves him right!

Then while the attention is on Marcus, I take the chance to have a sneaky glance at ⊙ ⊂⊃ Amy's paper and memorize a few answers. (At least this way I will definitely get some right.)

Then I carry on with my drawings. (I'll show them to Derek later.) This math lesson is turning out to be quite good after all.
RESULT! ☺

MR. KEEN is head of Oakfield School. He likes to "POP" into classes to see what we're up to.

Today he decides to say hello to Class 5F (us). Luckily I have some impressive-looking math in front of me. (Thanks mostly to Amy.)

"Hello, Class 5F."

"Hello, Mr. Keen."

Mr. Keen then launches into the usual type of headmaster "chat."

While he does that, here are a few interesting

FACTS about Mr. Keen.

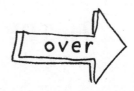

over

1. He has a very RED face that gets redder when he gets cross.

2. Mr. Keen gets cross quite easily.

Here's a RED-O-METER that shows clearly the different stages of redness Mr. Keen's face goes through.

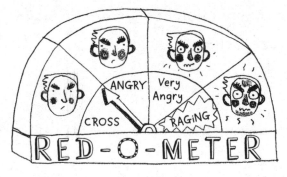

ANGRY Very Angry

CROSS RAGING

RED-O-METER

3. Mr. Keen's eyebrows look like two HAIRY Caterpillars crawling across his face.

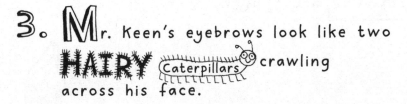

Mr. Keen is still chatting when my stomach starts to make really LOUD grumbly hungry noises (it's nearly lunchtime). I'm hoping he might take the hint and stop talking. But he carries on.

When my stomach growls again I pretend it's not me by staring at Marcus.

The bell goes off for lunch but Mr. Keen still keeps rambling on and on.

"I'll let you all go to lunch now,"
he says.

(ABOUT TIME.)

There's a trick to rushing down to the cafeteria without looking like you're *PUSHING* anyone out of the way. Very fast walking does the trick.

Fast walking

I grab my lunch box and try not to take in the smell of the ⌇⌇⌇⌇⌇⌇⌇

U.F.O.S

(**U**nidentified **F**ood **O**bjects)

 that are being served.

On Mondays, Tuesdays, and Wednesdays I bring my lunch. On Thursdays and Fridays I have school food.

This is because on Thursdays AMY PORTER has school lunch and on Fridays it's FRIES.

Derek is already sitting at the table eating. So I sit next to him, and then Norman Watson sits next to me. When I open my lunch box there's a note inside from my Granny Mavis.

Enjoy!
Love
Granny
xx

(Oh, NO! I forgot. Granny likes to help out and make my packed lunch when she visits. And I wasn't there to stop her.)

La!
La!
La!

I'm really hoping that she hasn't actually tried to cook **anything odd** for me.

Looking ⊙ ⊙ in my lunch box, I can see something that looks a bit like a pizza.
It is a pizza.
(So far so good.)

Made in the shape of a face.
I think?

It's *my* face ... groan.

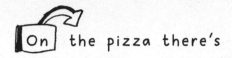 the pizza there's

cheese (OK),

tomatoes (OK),

olives (UGH).

And something else that I personally don't think should **EVER** in a

million years be seen on a pizza ... ever ...

La!

La!

La!

(What was Granny thinking?)

A BANANA!

There's a |banana| on my pizza.

I take it off really quickly before anyone sees that I have a banana on my pizza and thinks I'm weird.

Too late....

Amy and Florence walk past me and both pull a "that's disgusting" face at me and sit at another table.

Then Norman Watson nudges me and says,

"Is that a banana on your pizza?"

"Maybe ..." I say.

"YUM! I'll have it if you don't want it."

So I let Norman eat my banana and don't ask any questions.

Derek whispers,
"That's gross" to me. But Norman seems happy enough, so I keep quiet. I eat the rest of the pizza anyway. (It tastes a bit banana-ish in places.)

Granny Mavis has a few more unusual surprises for me lurking in my lunch box:

Cucumber juice in a can.

Lavender and potato biscuits.

And a lemon.   (Why?)

Derek has some more normal food for lunch, which he shares with me. (That's why he's my best mate.)

Best mate

We're just about to go out to break when Mrs. Mumble (that's her real name) makes an announcement over the loudspeaker. No one can ever understand what Mrs. Mumble says, so you have to listen carefully.

Hello! Will Tom Gates come to see Mrs. Worthington... Tom Gates..... Thank you!

I think she said Tom Gates to see Mrs.
Worthington?... She did.
I forgot about my detention.

GROAN.

I have to help Mrs. Worthington put up all
the portraits we did.
(Not the one I did of her, obviously.)

When she's not looking, I add a few extra
details to Marcus's portrait....

Which I think are a great improvement.

CLASS 5F SELF-PORTRAITS

Ross White

Paul Jolly

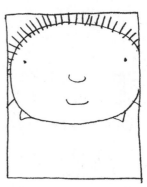

Solomon Stewart

Julia Morton

Norman Watson

Pansy Bennet

Mark Clump

Amber Tulley Green

Amy Porter

Trevor Peters

Brad Galloway

Leroy Lewis

Tom Gates

Florence Mitchell

Indrani Hindle

Marcus Meldrew

OH, NO. Mr. Fullerman's

been looking in my notebook.

Tom,
I'm sure **DOGZOMBIES** is a fantastic band.
But you need to concentrate on your **MATH**
in the future. (By the way, I like
this logo best.)

Mr. Fullerman

I make a huge effort to pay attention in
lessons, as I can't afford to get into any
more trouble. Especially if I want Dad to buy
DUDE3 tickets....

Even though I know that Mom and Dad will now use this at every opportunity to make me do stuff that I really don't want to do, like:

"Eat your vegetables ... if you want those DUDE 3 tickets."

"Clean up your room ... if you want those DUDE 3 tickets."

"Let your sister in the bathroom first ... if you want those DUDE 3 tickets."

I can hear them now.

This is not going to be easy.

I'm trying to be extra good in Mr. Fullerman's lesson.

I even volunteer to hand out the school field trip forms.

Marcus tries to grab his form from me straightaway.

I say "Manners" to him, then leave him until last. Making him reach for his form a few times is fun. Until Mr. Fullerman gives me one of his SCARY glares.

Teacher STARE

The trip actually looks like it could be quite good.

Year 5 class trip to the Museum to look at **the Egyptians and mummies**.

Dear Parent/Caregiver:

This term we will be studying the Egyptians and would like to take all the classes to the Museum as part of the project.

This will be for the whole day and the children will need a packed lunch. We will be traveling by bus and we will need parent helpers on the day if anyone is available.

Please fill in the form below, which gives your child permission to attend the trip.

Many thanks,

Mr. Fullerman

Tear off and return to school **ASAP**.

Child's Name Tom GATES Class 5F

I give permission for my child to go to the Museum

YES/NO ☺

Signed _Rita Gates_ Print Rita Gates
(good job!)

Does your child have any allergies? **Yes**
If so, what are they? Do not give Tom ANY vegetables
Are they taking any medicines? If so, what? Yes... cough sweets. Or just SWEETS would be fine

Are you able to help on the trip? No NoNo
Contact name ~~~~~~~~
Contact number ~~~~~~~~

(All done.)

Today Mr. Fullerman asks us to read out to the class our "What we did on summer holiday" stories. I feel happy about this because I got

five merits for mine.

It will be a good opportunity to impress Amy, hopefully.

Norman Watson reads his first.

He went to DISNEYLAND.
He's SO lucky! (But he didn't get five merits like me. Ha!)

Marcus Meldrew got sent away to summer camp for nearly the WHOLE HOLIDAY. I think he annoys his parents as much as he annoys me. (I'd send him away for the whole year if I could.)

Julia Morton's "I found an interesting shell" story is not interesting at all.

This lesson is starting to get a bit dull when Mark Clump stands up and reads "MY NEW PET SNAKE," which gets my attention.

He tells us about the mice he keeps in the freezer to feed the snake.

And how he bought the snake, where it lives, what the snake is called (Snakey . . . not very original). It's a really good story.

And the BEST part about the whole story is when he reaches inside his desk and brings out . . . .

It's awesome. But Mr. Fullerman doesn't think so. Neither does half the class, who run out. SCREAMING

Mr. Fullerman makes Mark put his snake away. The school office rings his mom, who comes to pick them both up. Which is a shame, because I really like snakes and I didn't get to see it properly.

At the end of school we get a note to take home.

Dear Parent/Caregiver,

Please can we remind all children and parents that NO PETS of any kind can be brought into school.

Pets are for home, not for the classroom. Especially pets that can be considered slightly scary (like snakes).

Thank you,

Mr. Keen
Headmaster

Speaking of pets, Derek is getting a new pet DOG. I can't wait! Delia is allergic to dogs, so I'm not allowed to get one. But Derek can bring his dog over ALL the time because:

1. I really like dogs.

2. Delia will be forced to stay in her room or she'll have to go out. Either way she won't be around to annoy me.

Perfect!

Derek's Dog

Derek sends me a photo of his dog.

This weekend the whole family is having lunch at the old **FOSSILS'** house.

Mom is stressed about what we'll be eating, especially since I mentioned my banana pizza.

Dad is stressed because his brother (my uncle Kevin) and his family will be there. Uncle Kevin seems to know a lot of things. Dad says it's because he's a "know-it-all."

Auntie Alice always laughs at Uncle Kevin's jokes, even when they're not funny (which is most of the time).

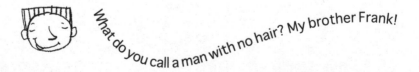

What do you call a man with no hair? My brother Frank!

Ha, Ha! Ha!

Delia is in a bad mood because she doesn't want to go. I say, "Delia's got a boyfriend, Delia's got a boyfriend," which puts her in an even WORSE mood.

Mom and Dad say she HAS to come.

Something tells me this lunch isn't going to be much fun.

Luckily the Fossils are in a VERY good mood and happy to see everyone, which helps a lot.

Yo! kids!

Hello!

My twin cousins are already there (and eating ... they eat loads). They are even taller than Solid. I say "Hi" to them. They don't talk much; they just wave at me.

Mom asks what we're eating for lunch today. We all listen nervously.

Granny announces we're having:

Chicken stuffed with cheese.

Roasted eggs?

Peas on a stick.

I really hope it tastes better than it sounds.

We're all sitting at the table when Uncle Kevin asks Dad if he's gotten balder, which makes Auntie Alice laugh.

Ha, Ha!

Dad doesn't look too happy.

Granny steps in and asks,

"Is everything OK?"

We all say, "Yes!"

"Delicious!" "Mmmmm!"

And nice things like that. But I notice no one is eating very much apart from the cousins. And Delia is secretly texting under the table.

Uncle Kevin starts talking about their

"AMAZING three-week holiday in

 Greece."

So I tell everyone about our terrible two-day

camping holiday and how it rained

and the tent was washed away

because Dad STUPIDLY put the tent

up by the stream. And then how I fell out of

the tree....

Auntie Alice and Uncle Kevin seem to be

enjoying the story. Ha, Ha! Ha, Ha!

Mom and Dad are GLARING at me in

a "BE QUIET" kind of way.

Granddad changes the subject and asks me

about my band.

So I tell him about **DOG ZOMBIES**, and then I tell everyone that **DUDE 3** is coming to play in our town!

"Dad is SO brilliant, he's promised to buy tickets for us to see them," I say.
(Dad looks surprised but doesn't say no.)

I'm a genius.

BEST DAD

Turns out that the cousins are HUGE fans of **DUDE 3**, too. It's the most excited I've seen them since they won a chocolate fountain at their school fair.

Uncle Kevin suggests we all go together on a "big family night out." I don't mind who I go with as long as it's not just Delia. So I say "GREAT!" But Dad doesn't look pleased at all with the idea. Especially when Uncle Kevin starts going on about Dad's "terrible taste in music when we were growing up."

Dad is just about to say something to Uncle Kevin when Granny bursts into the room with ...

"PUDDING!"

She has to explain what it is, because no one can tell.

It's a MASSIVE pile of bright pink pancakes that taste OK but look like horrid raw bits of liver.

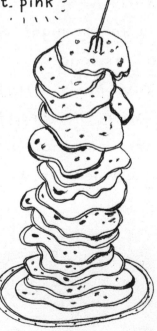

On the way home, we stop off for fish and chips  because everyone is still hungry.

M om and D ad don't seem happy.

D elia is miserable (no change there, then).

B ut I am VERY happy because:

1. I'm definitely going to see **DUDE 3** now.

2. Granny gave me some candy and some money on the way out.

RESULT! Can't WAIT to tell Derek.

(All I have to do now is ask **Amy** to the concert.)

Today I was only a tiny bit late for school. Hiding Delia's sunglasses took slightly longer than usual. Slipping them into an open bag of salad was inspired, I thought. Delia would NEVER have found them if Mom hadn't been making sandwiches.

I got out of the house before Delia or Mom got the chance to tell me off.

Just crept into class in time for attendance.

Mr. Fullerman looks up from the attendance list

and asks me why I'm late. I do what anyone would do in my position: blame my older sister for locking me in the bathroom.

Mr. Fullerman makes a note of my excuse on the attendance list, then moves on.

PHEW!

AMY PORTER isn't the slightest bit interested in my excuses because she is too busy memorizing her

SPELLING!

(OH! NO! NOT the spelling test.) This is <u>not</u> a good start to the day. I'm panicking and wondering how I'm going to get through this when something brilliant happens. I look over at Mr. Fullerman's desk and I *think* I can see all the answers to this week's spelling test. The paper is turned over, but I can make out what the words are backwards. And copy them down quickly before anyone notices.

Like this.

(This test will be easy-peasy now!)

Bananas
Areas
Cameras
Radios
Umbrellas
Piano
Solo
Fiesta
Plastic

(What I can see.)

Bananas
Areas
Cameras
Radios
Umbrellas
Piano
Solo
Fiesta
Plastic

(What I write down.)

Mr. Fullerman begins the test. I'm pretending to think carefully and write them down. And straightaway I realize there's a very BIG problem.

These spelling words are not the same as Mr. Fullerman's. Which makes me think I've written down next week's test instead.

I'm panicking, my mind's gone blank, and I've missed the first THREE spellings already. FOUR spellings ... FIVE spellings ... SIX-SEVEN-EIGHT ... the whole test. I keep pretending to write, so Mr. Fullerman doesn't suspect anything, and hope for the best. IF Mr. Fullerman spots that I already have next week's test, he might smell a rat!

cheat

The test is over and we have to swap papers with the person next to us so they can mark them. Marcus hands me his paper.

Oh, dear. I'm in trouble now.

I have to think quickly....

AGH!

Disaster has struck in the shape of a leaking pen.

Mr. Fullerman makes me clean up my ink "accident." WHOOPS!

I get to check Marcus's test.
He thinks he's done very well and is looking extra smug.

Marcus Meldrew

1. potaoe ☹ ✗
2. Volcano ✓
3. Tattwo ☹ ✗
4. Kangeroow ✗
5. Hero ✓
6. Igloow ✗
7. Echo ✓
8. Mangoe ✗ $\frac{3}{8}$

Only 3/8 for **M**arcus.

Not so smug now.

Amy got 8/8 (she's so smart).

I say "WOW! Well done, Amy." (It's winding Marcus up.) "You're SO good at spelling, aren't you?"
Then Amy says, "Thanks ... but I can't draw like you can." (She actually said something nice to me!)

So while the class is checking the spelling, I show Amy my latest DOGZOMBIE drawings and ask her to pick the best one. (She chooses the same one as Mr. Fullerman.)

This is the longest conversation I have ever had with Amy. I tell her about **DUDE3** and how they're playing in our town.

And it turns out that Amy REALLY likes them, too, which is BRILLIANT!

I'm trying to think about the best way to invite Amy to see **DUDE3** when she says she likes singing.

I say, "I like singing, too." Then she says, "Really?" And I say,

"YES, I can't get enough of singing."

So she suggests I join the school choir (like her) and I hear myself say,

"That's a **great** idea, I'd LOVE to join the choir."

(WHY? WHY? WHY did I say that?)

Which is exactly what Derek says when I tell him,

"I'm joining the choir. It will be good for my singing and the band."

"You think so?" (Derek is not convinced.)

Derek

(No, I don't think so. But I'm hoping Amy will come and see **DUDE 3** and I can't tell Derek that.)

I pass a choir practice poster on the school notice board. And I can't believe rehearsals are at LUNCHTIME! I don't even get to miss a boring lesson or two.
I'll go maybe once or twice to keep Amy happy, then drop out later on.

Good plan.

School Assembly

It's a "special assembly" today.

I can't believe that MARCUS is getting an award for his vacation homework! This seems very unfair as I got 5 merits as well.

Mr. Keen, our headmaster, gives out the prizes in front of the whole school.

It will be sick -making to watch Marcus being ultra smug. To make it worse, Mr. Fullerman asks Marcus to take the attendance list to the school office. Marcus thinks he's something special.

(While he's out of the class, I decide to add my own comments to his work.)

smug

Mr. Keen is standing in front of the
whole school.

He is telling us the usual sort of things that
headmasters like to say.

**"Lots of hard work . . ." "Looking forward
to . . ."** Blah, Blah, Blah.

I'm sitting behind SOLID,
so I can't see much of what's
going on.

Mrs. Nap leads the school in a rendition of "Morning Has Broken."

She is another one of those very enthusiastic teachers who *SWAYS* a lot from side to side while singing at the top of her voice.

Pansy Bennet  (don't mess with Pansy, she's tough) and of course Marcus are both getting awards.

Brad Galloway (who has cool hair ) is next to me. I tell him to keep his eyes peeled on Marcus.

"Sssshhhhhhh."

Mr. Fullerman is giving me the beady eye now.

 BEADY eyes

Mr. Keen says,

"Today we have some very important prizes to give out. Will Treasure Alexander and Grace Cole come up and get their certificates for good work on their shared nature project."

We all clap while the girls show everyone
their impressive project.

**"Will Pansy Bennet and Marcus Meldrew
come up with their excellent 'My
Summer Vacation' homework?"**

Pansy holds her book up. It has some nice-
looking writing and drawings in it. Everyone
claps. Then she takes her certificate.
Next Marcus holds his work up to show the
school. He's parading it around so the whole
school can see what's written in his book.

Everyone bursts out laughing. And they keep laughing.

MY Holiday

I Am an IDIOT

Ha! Ha! Ha! Ha! Ha! Ha! Ha! Ha! Ha! Ha! Ha! Ha! Ha! Ha! Ha! Ha! Ha! Ha!

(I enjoy the moment.)

Marcus takes a certificate and sits back down quickly. He's still wondering why everyone was laughing at him.

I wish all assemblies were this much fun, because for a short time, I forget all about promising to join the choir. It's only when assembly's over and I walk past that poster again that it all comes flooding back to me....

Groan.

cross

Mr. Fullerman is not in a good mood now either. (He suspects I had something to do with "adding" to Marcus's work.)

He reminds me about my review and tells us about the school concert. (The choir will be singing, apparently.)

And if that's not enough, he gives us a sign-up form for parents' evening.

How am I supposed to fit in band practice now?

I manage to get through the rest of the lesson by concentrating VERY hard on two things.

1. What I'm going to eat for lunch.

2. The small black fly trying to land on Mr. Fullerman's round head.

It takes a while, but the fly gets there in the end. And Mr. Fullerman says,

"Glad to see you're paying such close attention to me, Tom."

Which makes me laugh. Then Amy mentions "choir practice at lunchtime."

"Great," I say. "Can't wait."

(Groan.)

Mrs. **N**ap welcomes the new faces (me) to the choir. I never knew **SOLID** was in the choir (he kept that quiet), and OH, **NO** ... Marcus is here, too. Great, I can't get away from him.

Amy looks pleased to see me, so that's something.

Mrs. **N**ap puts me right next to Marcus ...

AGAIN.

She begins by making us do ridiculous warm-up exercises for our voices. We pull lots of silly faces and make odd noises. Then we learn the songs for the concert. Which is surprisingly fun. I'm *almost* starting to enjoy myself.

Mrs. Nap asks us all to sway from side to side when we're singing.

We're supposed to all sway together in the same direction. But Marcus keeps swaying (accidentally on purpose) into me. So I Sway into HIM.

Then he SWAYS into me and stamps on my foot. So I give him a BIG shove (which gets him off my foot).

Then he SWAYS into me AGAIN so I sway just that little bit too HARD into him. And Marcus goes flying onto the floor (as if he's been hit by an elephant!).

Now he's sniveling on the ground, shouting,

"Tom PUSHED ME.
TOM PUSHED ME!"
(He's SO annoying.)

Mrs. Nap helps Marcus up. Then sends ME out, saying,

"You should know better, Tom. Perhaps choir is not for you after all."

I thought I was doing SO well.

I draw a picture of Marcus, which makes me feel better.

Marcus is a slimy toad.

CROAK!

HISTORY

Back in class, Marcus is sitting as far away from me as possible. (Just as well, I say.)

"**M**arcus is an idiot," **A**my tells me. She saw him push me and tread on my foot. (Maybe choir practice was a good idea after all?)

While Amy is feeling a tiny bit sorry for me, I take the opportunity to ask her about **DUDE3**. (I remember Amy LOVES the band.)

"Are you going to see them?" I say.

"**I WISH**!" she tells me. "I don't have a ticket." Then Marcus (who just can't help himself because he is a nosy twit) butts in.

"I've got **V.I.P.** tickets."

His dad knows someone who knows someone who knows someone who has got them tickets.... Yawn.

I tell him **V.I.P.** stands for

Very Irritating Person.

And he believes me. Ha! Ha!

So I invite Amy to the concert with me and Derek, and my dad.
(I don't mention Uncle Kevin, Auntie Alice, and the cousins.) And she says "OK" and goes back to reading.

"BRILLIANT," I say, and that's it.

All sorted. We're all going to see my favorite band. That was easy. Then stupidly, I stop listening to the history lesson and imagine being at the concert instead (which is much more fun).

DUDE 3 is fantastic—playing all their great songs. Suddenly, in the middle of a

guitar solo, the  guitarist is taken
ill and has to be dramatically carried offstage.

The lead singer asks the crowd,
"*Does anyone know how to play*
DUDE 3 *songs?*"

"ME!" I shout and jump onstage. The
crowd cheers. Amy cheers. Derek cheers.
I start to play, and the crowd is amazed.
They begin to call my name.

TOM! *TOM!*

TOM!

TOM!

TOM!

Mr. Fullerman is shouting at me. (I've missed most of the history lesson.)

Worth it, though.

Will catch up tonight and get back into Mr. Fullerman's good books by not being late for the school trip tomorrow.

Which I'm really looking forward to now. 😊

School TriP

Mr. Fullerman is not pleased because I am LATE again. It was Delia's fault (well, that's what I tell Mr. Fullerman).

Everyone is already on the bus and very excited, especially Norman Watson, who keeps leaping up and down in his seat.

On the bus, I can only see one spare seat left, right next to ...

NO, not Mrs. Worthing"tash"!

Free seat

Hello, Tom!

Derek has already saved me a place by him. But he thinks it's funny to watch me panic.

"**Y**our face!" he laughs.
"Ha! Ha! Very funny," I say.

The bus journey takes **AGES** because some of the class needs to use the toilet and **Julia Morton** feels carsick (she's gone a nasty shade of green). So we have to keep stopping. Eventually we arrive at the museum.

It's **HUGE,** with big stone steps up to old wooden doors that have massive pillars either side. Lots of other schools are there (all better behaved than us).

We get split up into three groups with one teacher each (we've got Mrs. Nap).

We're all given an Egyptian Quiz to do. I'm in Amy's group with Derek, so we rush around the museum, mostly copying what Amy writes. The quiz doesn't take long, so we get to check out the gift shop early.

I know exactly what I want to buy.

At lunchtime SOMEONE (OK, me) gives Norman half a caramel wafer. (I forget that sugar makes Norman even more hyper than usual.)

We are all sitting listening to the Museum Egyptian Expert. She is showing us a real mummy and telling us in great **GORY** detail how the Egyptians would

"use a long hook to pull out the dead person's brain through their nose before mummifying them..."

Julia Morton goes green and feels sick again.

Norman can't sit still and wants to take a closer look at the mummy.

He JUMPS up a bit too quickly and

pushes Brad Galloway, who bumps into Leroy, who falls on SOLID, who accidentally shoves Mrs. Worthington. Then she falls over and knocks into a very rare Egyptian vase....

Thankfully, Mr. Fullerman manages to CATCH IT!

He's holding on to it really tightly and breathing a sigh of relief just when Julia Morton leans forward and is sick.

(I don't think that's what Egyptian vases were originally used for.)

The museum expert can't get rid of us quickly enough.

While Julia is getting cleaned up,
we all get to go to the gift shop again.
I buy some brilliant Egyptian tattoos.

On the way home the bus is much quieter because some kids have gone to sleep, including Marcus. Which is excellent news because:

1. I don't have to listen/talk to him (he's annoying).
2. I'm still cross he got me kicked out of choir practice.
3. It gives me a chance to try out my new Egyptian tattoos.

Which work great!

I am doing some more drawing, which gets me **THINKING** about some other interesting **STUFF....**

Moon Cookie

Rules:

Here are a few **rules** based on stuff that's happened to me (so it's all true).

RULE 1.

School photos are always **HIDEOUS**. It's the law, I think. Even if a world-famous photographer was to take a school photo, it would **STILL** be rubbish.

HIDEOUS
school
photo

RULE 2.

Your siblings (in my case, Delia) know ways to annoy you that nobody else does.

RULE 3.

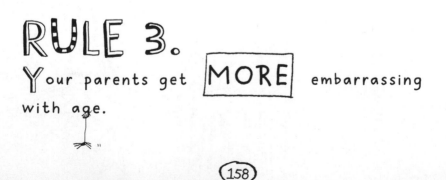

Your parents get **MORE** embarrassing with age.

My dad is now officially the

WORLD CHAMPION of embarrassing dads.

When we got back from the school trip, Dad
was there to pick me up.
He was wearing:
A nasty-colored pompom hat with his name
on it.

Muddy jeans tied up with a piece of string.

NO belt, just STRING.

A grubby shirt with holes and patches.

And filthy old Wellington boots.

"I've been gardening," he said.
  (Like that's an excuse!)
"Well, I won't bother to pick you up again."
(If only.)

Brad Galloway and Mark Clump both thought
he was a tramp.

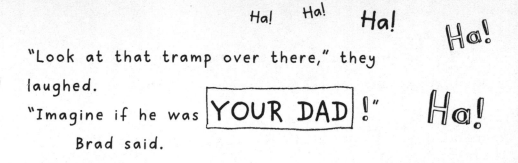

"Look at that tramp over there," they laughed.

"Imagine if he was YOUR DAD !" Brad said.

"He is my dad," I told them. I couldn't get home fast enough.

I only forgave Dad when he pulled out four (slightly muddy) DUDE3 tickets from his pocket.

BRILLIANT !

(That's why he came to pick me up.)

I'm officially excited now and very happy.

AT home Delia spoils everything by waving my school photo around and laughing at it. "FREAK photo or WHAT?"

Annoyingly, I have to agree. It's AWFUL, terrible, a really rotten, cheesy picture.

HIDEOUS
school
photo

I've got odd hair and a red face. I knew it would be bad, but not *that* bad.

AGHH!

I grab it back from her and try to hide it before Mom sees it. Delia says,

"TOO LATE, NERD BOY."

Apparently Mom loves it and has already ordered about a million copies for the entire family....

GROAN.

ToM'S School Photo

I tell Derek about the DUDE3 tickets. Derek tells me he's got his NEW PUPPY!! He's going to bring the puppy over to my house tonight for band practice so I can see it. (Also that will keep Delia away.)

Mr. Fullerman appears to be in a good mood. (Despite me only just making it to school on time ... *and* forgetting my review homework AGAIN.)

"Today we're going to be making models of pyramids."

(Which sounds like fun for a change.)

He puts us into groups. I'm with Norman, Amber, Pansy, Indrani, and SOLID. (I have to move tables.)

Solid has a good idea for the shape of the model.

"It should be sort of pyramid-shaped?"

GENIUS.

Indrani draws a card template, and Amber cuts it out. Then we all help to cover it in glue and paper, which makes a nice and sturdy model.

Everyone is working together really well (unusually for Class 5F). Our pyramid is actually starting to look a bit like ... a pyramid.

Mr. Fullerman's attention is on Mark Clump's group, who aren't doing so well.

Then Norman starts to get bored. (He gets bored easily.)

"Let's make a mummy," he suggests.

GREAT IDEA.

Norman gets six toilet paper rolls from the school toilet and tries to "wrap up" SOLID. But there's not enough paper to cover him (too big and tall). So we use Norman instead. He's smaller but a lot more fidgety.

"Keep still, Norman," I tell him.

It's not easy covering his legs and head with the TP. When he's finally mummified, Norman starts walking around with his arms stretched out (like a real mummy).

He makes WHOOOOOOOOOOOOOAAAAAA, WHOOOOOOOOOOOOOAAAAA! noises.

It's very realistic. He's good.

He's scaring Amber. AGH!

Mr. Fullerman looks over to see what we're up to.

SUDDENLY, Mr. Keen the headmaster bursts into the classroom.

(On one of his little visits.)

Norman is still behind the door. He doesn't move.

Mr. **K**een asks about the school trip and admires our pyramid work.

(WHHHHOOOOOOOOOOAA, WOOOOOOOOOOOOOAAA)

"What's that strange moaning noise?"

The class starts laughing.

(WHHHHOOOOOOOOOOOAA, WOOOOOOOOOOOOAAA)

"There it is again."

Mr. Keen's face starts to hover around the "getting cross" color on the **R**ed-**O**-**M**eter when he's called away by an announcement from **M**rs. **M**umble. And as Mr. Keen closes the door, everyone can now see Norman making

WHHHHOOOOOOOOOAA, WOOOOOOOOOOOOOOOAAA
noises and pretending to be a mummy.

Including Mr. Fullerman.
Who's not in such a good mood now.

WHHOOOOOOOOOOAAAAA,
WHHOOOOOOOOOOAAAAA

It's been an eventful
day at school.

(janitor Stan replacing toilet rolls →)

I can't wait to meet Derek's new PUPPY now! He's very cute (unlike Derek), although I can see a slight similarity from the picture he e-mailed me.

We let him run around my house .... into Delia's room. Where he chews a few pairs of sunglasses and jumps on her bed.

GOOD DOG!

Delia is furious.

But she has to keep her distance because she's allergic to dogs.

Derek and I are busy practicing some new DOG ZOMBIES tunes (Derek's dog is ~~singing~~ sorry, *howling* along)

oowwl

when Dad pops his head around the door. He wants to know if we need another guitarist for the band. (We don't.)

Hello!

He says things like that in a jokey kind of way. But sometimes I think he really means it. Dad reminds us about the concert next week.

Apparently Delia's not coming with us because she's going with "friends." (I think she has a boyfriend, which is a horrible thought.) At least she won't be able to spoil my fun like usual.

Uncle Kevin, Auntie Alice, and the twins are meeting us at the concert. I feel sorry for anyone who ends up standing behind the twins. They won't see a thing.

Can't see

Derek and I discuss wearing our T-shirts.

(Must check what Dad plans to wear just in case it's too embarrassing. It will be.)

TOM . . . where is your HOMEWORK?

Mr. Fullerman is in a really **BAD** mood today.

I keep forgetting to bring in my review homework.

I'm going to get another detention at this rate.

He's not pleased at all.

Plus we have parents' evening tonight (I forgot about THAT as well).

Now Mom and Dad will be the LAST parents to see Mr. Fullerman.

Because I didn't bring in my form. ☹
Being last will give them far too much time to look at my work and "chit-chat" with everyone (teachers and other parents—it will be awful).

Mr. Fullerman gives us today's work.

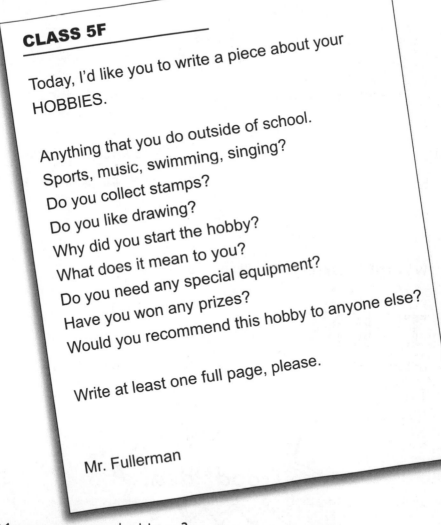

CLASS 5F

Today, I'd like you to write a piece about your HOBBIES.

Anything that you do outside of school.
Sports, music, swimming, singing?
Do you collect stamps?
Do you like drawing?
Why did you start the hobby?
What does it mean to you?
Do you need any special equipment?
Have you won any prizes?
Would you recommend this hobby to anyone else?

Write at least one full page, please.

Mr. Fullerman

Mmmmmm ... hobbies?

My hobbies are

😊 annoying Delia,

😊 being in a band,

😊 and eating caramel wafers.

I could write a whole page on annoying Delia, but I'm not sure that's what Mr. Fullerman had in mind.

What to write? What to write??

I KNOW—I'll make up a more interesting hobby for me to do. Something funny.

Good idea.

We spend most of the day sorting out our classroom and getting our books ready for parents' evening.

Marcus leaves his notebook out on his desk while he goes to the toilet.
(Mistake!)

I slip a few drawings I've done in between the pages of his work.
(That should make his parents' evening more interesting.)

PARENTS' EVENING

Mom and Dad (as predicted) are not happy that they'll be the last parents to see Mr. Fullerman.

It's always a bit weird coming back into school in the evening. Especially when the classroom is all clean and tidy (not like normal). Mr. Fullerman is wearing a suit and looks uncomfortable. Dad is wearing a terrible T-shirt, so I beg him to leave his jacket on.

SHAME

Mom insists on looking at EVERY piece of work up on the walls. Worse still, she keeps talking to teachers  that I don't have lessons with AND parents of kids I don't even know.

It's SO embarrassing!

I spot SOLID, who doesn't look happy (he looks JUST like his DAD, though).

"Parents' evening sucks," he whispers.

I agree.

Then I see Amy. Her parents are with Mr. Fullerman already. They are both smiling and laughing (no problems with Amy's work, then).

Dad says he's got Amy's **DUDE3** ticket in his pocket and he could give it to her "folks" now.

(Folks? Don't say folks, please?)

So we wait for them to finish. Then Dad strikes up a conversation with Amy's dad about **MUSIC** in a really **LOUD** voice.

Amy rolls hers eyes and looks at me.
"Sorry," I say, and we both have to stand there and wait for our parents to stop embarrassing us. They chat for ages about all kinds of rubbish.
Then Dad forgets to give them the ticket after all that!

Finally, when **M**r. Fullerman has seen all the other parents, it's our turn ... groan.

He brings out a folder that's full of letters.

← Tom's letters

"Can I start with Tom's letters from home?" he says.

Mom and Dad look a bit puzzled.

Not the LETTERs, NO!!

(I've been rumbled.)

Dear Mr. Fullerman,

Poor Tom has a cold and can't do sports outside
. . . ever.

Love from

Rita Gates

Dear Mr. Fullerman,

Please can Tom be excused from spelling this week. He's had a difficult week (family stuff).

Thanks,

Rita Gates

Dear Mr. Fullerman,

Tom has been helping his sick grandmother and has not been able to do his homework.

Sorry,

Rita Gates

Dear Mr. Fullerman,

Tom's delayed homework was due to his sister being nasty to him and not letting him use the computer. We have told her off.

Thanks,

Frank Gates

Dear Mr. Fullerman,

Tom has been helping his sick grandfather and has not been able to do his homework.

Whoops,

Frank Gates

Dear Mr. Fullerman,

Please can Tom be excused from swimming?
He is allergic to ~~water~~ chemicals in the water.

Thank you,

Rita Gates

It's not a good start to parents' evening.
(What can I say? It worked for a while.)

But the good news is, I'm doing well in ART
and English.

Spelling is only so-so. Could improve at math.
Could do better at science and history. Good
at P.E.

It's not all bad.

Room for improvement, Mr. Fullerman says.

They have a nice chat about me (like I'm not
there).

Chat,
chat.

Tom
this,
Tom
that.

I smile and agree not to:

1. ☺ Chat so much. ☺

2.  so much.

3. ☺ Fake letters from home again.

Generally I'm an OK kid.

It's a *reasonably* good parents' evening.
Then Mom and Dad both read

"MY NEW HOBBY" (which I completely
forgot about). And it all goes HORRIBLY
wrong.
From the looks on their faces I can see
they're not happy.

MY NEW HOBBY

By Tom Gates

My mom and dad like to use my pocket money as an extra way of making me do things I'm not very keen on doing.

For instance:

"Clean up your room ... or no pocket money."

"Eat your vegetables ... or no pocket money."

"Be nice to your sister ... or no pocket money."

(Which I think is possibly against my human rights?) And if that's not bad enough, Dad seems to take great pleasure in placing my money in very high places. Like doors, shelves, and anywhere I can't easily reach it.

HIGH

Wh en I do finally get my hands on it,
Mom often borrows it back to buy
milk and newspapers. Emergency money, she says.

I discovered my new hobby completely by
accident.

Fed up listening to Mom and Mrs. Fingle
(Derek's mom) "chit-chatting" outside the shops
(for what seems like HOURS), I sit on the
pavement and look
really bored Chit-chatting   Mrs. Fingle
(my legs
ache, too). When someone walks past me, he
drops some money into my lap.

Real money!

It's BRILLIANT!

(I think they must feel SORRY for me!)

So I put on an even *sadder* face, and
someone else gives me another $1.
By the time Mom and Mrs. Fingle have finished
talking, I've made $3.70 all on my own.
Which gets me thinking. What if I use a
SHAKILY written sign like

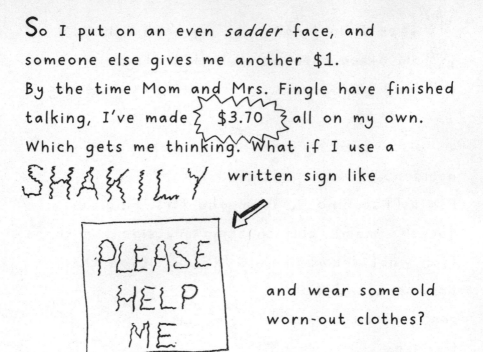

PLEASE
HELP
ME

and wear some old
worn-out clothes?

So I give that a go, too, and sure enough I
make even MORE money.

The great thing about my new hobby is you
can do it anywhere and you get to meet

LOTS of different people. And now I don't have to rely on Mom and Dad for my pocket money anymore. It's a hobby I would recommend to **EVERYONE**.

I am also in a band called

But we don't make any money at all (yet).

The End

"YOU'VE BEEN BEGGING?

BEGGING!

I CAN'T BELIEVE IT!"

Mom and Dad keep looking ⊙ ⊙ at me and shaking their heads.

(I wasn't begging; it's just a STORY.)

On the way home, they remind me again that "**NOT** everyone is as lucky as you, Tom." And "Begging is no joke!"

I'm trying to convince them that I was not begging. I tell them I was using my imagination.

I would NEVER beg. EVER!

"It was just a story! You know, pretending ... ha, ha, ha?"

I think they believe me now. Phew.

D̲elia hears Mom and Dad talking about my parents' evening and how they thought I'd been begging.

S̲he suddenly comes over and offers me a caramel wafer. E̲ven though I KNOW she's up to something, I STUPIDLY go to take it.

"I hear you're good at begging? Beg for the wafer, then," she says, and wafts the wafer in front of me. I want that wafer SO badly that I actually say "PLEASE." And she says, "SAY PRETTY PLEASE." So I say, "PRETTY PLEASE."

(It's so humiliating.)

"**I** can't hear you!"

"**PRETTY PLEASE!**"

Then, to my surprise, Delia actually hands over the wafer and goes off laughing.

It's only when I try to open the wafer that I realize that I have fallen for the old "empty wafer wrapper" trick.

Very funny, Delia.

Empty

Very funny.

I suddenly feel inspired to write a new song. When Derek comes over later, I show him a new song I've just written for

DOG
ZOMBIES

He likes it a
LOT!

Delia's a Weirdo

Who's that weirdo over there?
Dressed in **bLack**
With greasy hair
You can't trust her
She's not nice
She's got no heart ✗✗
Just a block of ice

CHORUS

Delia
She's a WEIRDO
Delia
She's a GEEK
Delia
She's a WEIRDO
Delia
She's a FREAK

Delia's a grumpy moo
Don't let her
Stand next to you
Big black glasses
Hide her eyes
She really smells
And that's no lie

CHORUS

BACK at School

Tom, I'm still waiting for your **HOMEWORK**.

(I got carried away practicing "Delia's a Weirdo." It's sounding really good. I have written a few more good verses. Will have to do homework **TONIGHT** ☾ ✳ ✳

before the **DUDE3** concert.)

I'm SO excited I can hardly concentrate.

Marcus is going on and on and **On** about his **V.I.P.** tickets.

v.i.p. v.i.p.
v.i.p. v.i.p.

"Shut up, Marcus." Even Amy is fed up with him.

Mr. Fullerman reminds us that **DUDE3** is not the only concert coming up. (How did he know about **DUDE3** ?).

"Don't forget about the SCHOOL CONCERT,"

he tells us.

When **M**r. Fullerman starts the lesson, I'm trying to work out how many hours it will be before the concert starts.

LOADS ... too many.

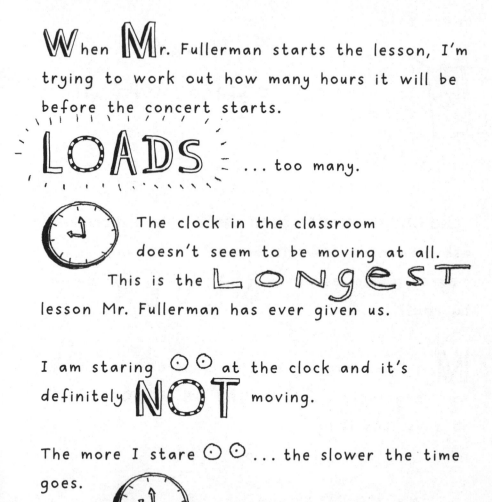

The clock in the classroom doesn't seem to be moving at all. This is the **LONGEST** lesson Mr. Fullerman has ever given us.

I am staring ⊙ ⊙ at the clock and it's definitely **NOT** moving.

The more I stare ⊙ ⊙ ... the slower the time goes.

And Mrs. Mumble keeps interrupting the lesson with announcements that no one can understand.

HELLO can : Please come follow the office. Mr Fullerman
|| `Thank you'!

"Did anyone understand that?" Mr. Fullerman asks. Then she says it again, but it's no clearer. (This lesson is NEVER going to end!)

Mr. Fullerman leaves the classroom to check what's going on. **"It might be important,"** he says. (As if.)
While he's gone, I have a

BRAINWAVE!

I stand on the table and MOVE the hands on the clock **forward** so the lesson is nearly finished. (This goes down well with my classmates.)

Hooray, hooray!

HOORAY!

Mr. Fullerman looks slightly confused when he comes back. He checks his own watch. **"Is the clock fast?"**

"NO, MR. FULLERMAN."

"Has anyone touched the clock?"

"NO, MR. FULLERMAN."

He notices the clock is slightly wonky on the wall. Mr. Fullerman is not convinced. He stands on a chair to put the clock back to the right time.

Just as Mrs. Mumble makes another announcement. It makes Mr. Fullerman jump, and he wobbles off the chair and onto the floor.

It's a DISαsTER!

(We'll **never** get out of this lesson at this rate.)

Not that I'm being unsympathetic. But this is turning out to be the longest lesson EVER.

Mr. Fullerman is wincing in pain and takes TWICE as long to do or say anything. And the rest of the day doesn't go any faster.

(It's like someone knows it's the concert tonight and is deliberately slowing the world down.)

MATH is a drag. P.E. takes forever. I'm getting changed out of my P.E. kit in the locker room when there is another really loud noise that starts

 BLARING

out of the speakers.

(Not Mrs. Mumble this time.
Something even LOUDER.)

Mr. Fullerman says it's a

FIRE ALarm DRILL!

"Leave everything and exit in an orderly fashion. DON'T RUN! Go outside."

I manage to grab my shoes and follow everyone else outside to the playground. Even though we have to **wait** for attendance to be taken and wait for all the other classes to come out. Time suddenly seems to be *FLYING* by. Mainly because Marcus has left his pants behind and is standing in the playground in just his briefs. Mrs. Nap gives him a sweater to tie around his waist. Now it looks like he's wearing a skirt.

It's the **FUNNIEST** thing I've seen in ages.

Mr. Fullerman says we can all go home
slightly early now. HOORAY!

Shame!

I'm telling Derek all about
what happened to Marcus on
the way home (especially the
sweater/skirt bit), when he
tells me he's got a proper
name for his dog now.

I try to guess what it is.

"Rocky?"

"Rover?"

"Fang?"

"It's ROOSTER," he says.

"ROOSTER? That's a kind of chicken, isn't it?
You're naming your dog after a chicken?"
(I suppose I'll get used to it.)

DUDE 3 HERE WE COME!

CLUCK

199

DUDE 3 CONCERT

Derek has brought Rooster over and he's running around our house looking for Delia. She's already gone to meet her friend (boyfriend, more likely). Derek and I are wearing our DUDE 3 T-shirts and looking cool.

Dad is wearing another terrible T-shirt and horrid pants. He <u>doesn't</u> look cool.

Mom agrees with me and makes him change. "And no crowd surfing," she tells Dad as we leave the house.

Change.

Then DAD remembers the tickets were in his other pants. So he goes back to get them. But he can't find them **ANYWHERE**.

THIS IS DREADFUL.

Don't panic.

I PANIC!

Derek is trying not to panic. We look around the whole house. In Delia's room, my room, the kitchen.

"Don't worry, they're here somewhere," he says. He checks his pockets. The bedrooms, the bathroom. We are officially **FRANTIC**. Where are the tickets?

YAP! YAP! YAP! YAP! YAP!

Rooster is running around chasing us from room to room. It's really annoying because he is barking and yapping and it's making everyone stressed.

Mom sends Rooster out to the garden. I'm checking my room again when I look out of the window and see Rooster playing with some bits of paper. The bits of paper look like they could have been ...

THE TICKETS!

"BAD ROOSTER!" Derek is saying. But it's too late. The tickets are all mangled and covered in teeth marks and dog drool.

"I'll stick them together," Dad says. "It'll be fine."

But it's not fine. The tickets are ruined .

"Maybe Uncle Kevin and Auntie Alice will sell us their tickets?" Dad says.

"Don't bank on it," Mom says.

"We'll think of something," Dad says.

But I'm too STUNNED to say anything at all.

We go to the show anyway.

"I'm never going to get a dog," I say to Derek. Which is a bit unfair, I know, because it's not his fault. I'm just really angry with his stupid chicken dog. GGGGGGGGGrrrrrrrrrrrrrr.

BAD Rooster

my is already there waiting with her dad.
"Let's see if they'll take the tickets anyway?"
says Dad. The man at the door takes one look
at the bits of ticket and shakes his head.

**"Sorry, pal. Can't take these,
they're all mashed up."**

Just when things couldn't get any worse...
Marcus and his dad turn up clutching four
V.I.P. tickets. Turns out that they now have
two spare V.I.P. tickets. And
Marcus's dad suggests that
we could have them. (Marcus
doesn't take after his dad,
who seems quite nice.)

Marcus's
Dad →

V.I.P. Tickets

I want to go SO badly. But my DAD says that
Amy and Derek should go. "Because we might
be able to get in with Uncle Kevin."
I am VERY ⊙ ⊙ brave. I tell Amy and
Derek that I really don't mind and that I'll be
fine. Then I watch all four of them go off to
the concert. (Inside I can't believe Derek and

Amy have gone with MARCUS!)

This is terrible.

Uncle Kevin and Auntie Alice are waving and calling Dad. Uncle Kevin is looking particularly pleased with himself. Dad tells him what's happened and how we can't get in now with the mangled tickets. Uncle Kevin says, (TYPICAL YOU!) which makes Dad cross. Uncle Kevin (being a salesman) has actually sold their tickets for three times as much as he paid for them. He's very happy and they're going to dinner instead of the concert. (I think the cousins would rather have seen the band.)

Great, this is turning into a nightmare. I'll NEVER get to see my favorite band now. Dad sees I'm **REALLY** upset.

"**S**tay here, don't move," he says. "I'll get some tickets, don't you worry, Tom."

I'm SO miserable.

I sit on the floor and look really fed up. The concert is about to start and we've got no chance of seeing them at this rate.

Then I have an idea.

It's a long shot, but I've got NOTHING to lose.

I'm desperate.

I find a paper bag, and I
already have a pen.

Then I get writing and
drawing.

I'm attracting a bit of attention, but no tickets as yet.

A lady walks past and says "Poor you," which is nice.

Then I'm suddenly aware of a man in leather pants reading my note.

He's shaking his head and looking at me.

I put on an extra SAD face.

Then he starts walking toward me and there's something very familiar about him.
I'm sure I've seen him before.
Then he asks me a question.

"Is this your new hobby, Tom?"
he asks, and it SUDDENLY dawns on me who it is....

BLIMEY, it's MR. FULLERMAN.

AGH! → LEATHER PANTS!

AND HE he's wearing leather pants! What's doing here? It's a terrible moment, bumping into a TEACHER outside of school. You don't really think of them having a life outside of being a teacher.

It's a shock (especially the leather pants).

Dad comes back, with no tickets.
He's NOT pleased to see me begging.

YOU'RE BEGGING?

"You told me it was a made-up story, Tom!"
"It was.... I was desperate!" I say.
"Stop begging right now! There must be
another way to see DUDE3 ."

Then Mr. Fullerman says,
**"Hello, Mr. Gates. I think I might be
able to help."**

And Dad looks as shocked as I am
to see it's Mr. Fullerman (wearing
leather pants).

I'm wondering what Mr. Fullerman is doing at
a DUDE3 show in the first place. And guess
what?

Turns out that Mr. Fullerman actually went to school MATES with DUDE3'S MANAGER!

They are good friends.

(Mr. Fullerman is NOT just a crusty old teacher after all.)

He speaks to someone backstage who gives us all special passes.

Thanks, man.

No problem. Nice pants.

SQUEAK!

NOW I can watch the whole show from the side of the stage!

I would HUG Mr. Fullerman if he wasn't my teacher (and wearing leather pants).

It's the BEST view ever!

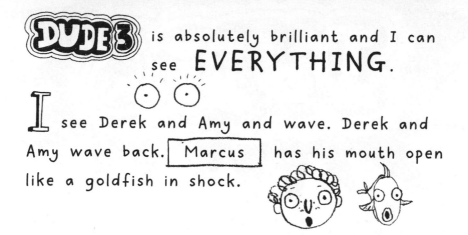

DUDE 3 is absolutely brilliant and I can see **EVERYTHING**.

I see Derek and Amy and wave. Derek and Amy wave back. | Marcus | has his mouth open like a goldfish in shock.

(It's almost the best part of the show. Ha, ha!)

Then I spot Delia in the audience. She's with her boyfriend. So I point him out to Dad and stir things up by saying he's got a VERY bad reputation around town.

What a fantastic night I'm having. **DUDE 3** play all their best songs.

Then right at the end ... it gets better ...

(I'll never wash again.)

I'm still buzzing when I get home.

Dad has forgotten about my begging (phew).

He's too busy worrying about Delia's dodgy boyfriend.

I go to bed **happy** and relive the whole gig in my head.

This is probably the

In the morning, Delia is slopping around the house sulking and being miserable.  Grrrrrrrr

Apparently it's all my fault because Mom and Dad want to meet her new "friend" now. (I am a GENIUS.)

Dad is humming **DUDE 3** songs at breakfast. mmmmmmmmmm

Mom is wearing a **DUDE 3** T-shirt.

It's SO embarrassing (old people trying to be trendy). I can't get out of the house quick enough.

Derek and I go to school together.

He's SO wishing he'd stuck with me at the concert now.

Seeing Mr. Fullerman again in "teacher" mode is *REALLY* weird.

The first thing he asks me is,

"WHERE'S YOUR HOMEWORK, TOM?"

"I was at the concert, sir, remember?"

Mr. Fullerman says that's no excuse and I'll get a detention unless I bring it in first thing in the morning, which is a bit harsh!

(He's SO back in teacher mode.)

With all the excitement about DUDE3, I completely forget about the school concert, which apparently is

TODAY.

I'm not worried because I'm not in it.

(No choir, which is a relief.) Phew.

Mrs. Nap is looking for helpers to put chairs out in the hall.

Helpers get to miss class,

so I volunteer.

All I have to do is show the little kids what to do. HOW hard is that?

We get all the chairs out when they start to mess around. I get TOUGH and suggest a quick game of musical ♫ ♪ chairs, which keeps them happy. There's no music—so I Sing my DOGZOMBIES Song

"Delia's a Weirdo."

It's all going VERY well. The little kids all join in and sing along with me.

"Delia, she's a weirdo!

Delia, she's a freak!" (Very catchy chorus.)

Then I sing the verse ...

221

and that's when Mr. Keen pops his head round the door to see how we're doing.

We all pretend to be arranging the chairs. (Little kids learn fast.)

"That's a jolly song, Tom," he says.

"Really, Mr. Keen?"

"Are you performing in the concert today?"

"No, Mr. Keen."

"Why not? You should be! I'll have a word with Mrs. Nap to give you a slot at the end."

"No, Mr. Keen, it's fine.... Really, I don't want to sing."

"Nonsense, that sounded excellent. Don't you agree, children?"

And all the little kids cheer and say,

"YES!"

Groan ... that's ALL I need. This could be very humiliating.
CORRECTION. It WILL be very humiliating.

I don't think Mr. Keen heard all the lyrics to the **DOG ZOMBIES** song, either.

Fool

"ARE YOU MAD?

Of course I DON'T want to play in the school concert!" Derek says.

NO WAY!

He thinks **DOGZOMBIES** have to plan their first gig very carefully.

(In other words, we're still a bit rubbish and need more practice.)

BUT he does come up with a BRILLIANT

plan that will get me off the hook and save me from serious humiliation.

The ONLY good thing about the school concert is we get to go home early to "prepare." (Eat caramel wafers, in my case.)

Mom says,  "What do you mean there's a school concert tonight?"

(I forgot to tell them.)

"And you're in it?"

"Sort of ..." I say.

Mom and Dad planned to meet Delia's dodgy "boyfriend" tonight.

"I'm not leaving them here on their own," Dad says. "They'll both have to come to the concert, too."

Ha, Ha! Delia will be delighted!

A romantic night out ... at my school concert.

She'll be so cross it's almost worth being in the concert.

Derek and I run through our plan one last time on the way back to school.

It has to work or I'll be stuffed.

Back at school, the hall is already packed with people. Mom and Dad sit at the back, which is a relief because Mom has on her DUDE 3 T-shirt and Dad is wearing gardening gear. ← Patches

Delia and her "boyfriend" look jolly (NOT).

Derek and I run through our plan one last time (I hope it works).

The lights go down and the concert begins.
First, there's some (slightly boring) poetry.

The star was bright.
We got a big fright.
That night.

Then we have to sit through some songs

and, of course, the choir.
Watching Marcus and
Solid SWAYING from side
to side is hilarious.

Amy is very good (of course).

Swaying

There's a play by Year
Three. (Quite funny.)
And a dance by Year Six.

(It's rubbish.)

AMY

Then Mr. Keen makes a speech about what a good term it's been ...
            blah, blah, blah.
And I hear him telling EVERYONE how he heard me singing and thought I should be in the concert.

It's AWFUL ... I can feel myself getting nervous and sweaty.

Now it's my turn.
Mr. Keen asks me what my song is called.

"'Delia's a Weirdo,'" I say.

Which makes everyone laugh ... apart from Delia, who's giving me the EVILS.

I sit on the stage and clear my throat.
  Everyone is looking at me and waiting.

So I clear my throat again ...

and wait ...
and wait ...

and strum a little (like I'm warming up).
(Mr. Keen is glaring at me now.)
So I'm thinking I might have to actually
start singing if Derek's plan doesn't work....

When at long LAST ...

A VERY Loud BLARING NoiSE goes OFF.

Mr. Fullerman tells everyone not to panic.
It's just the

FIRE ALARM!

We all have to leave the
hall straightaway.

The concert is abandoned.

RESULT!

Derek is a **GENIUS!** He gives me a THUMBS-UP as we leave school.
Better still ... Delia can hear some little children singing my song ...

DELIA, she's a weirdo! DELIA, she's a FREAK!

She's not happy, but her boyfriend is laughing. He won't be her boyfriend for long at this rate!

What's funny?

Mom and Dad think it's a shame I didn't get to do my song. (I don't!)

"Maybe next time, don't write about your sister, though," Mom tells me. "It only upsets her." (EXACTLY!)

Dad suggests writing about someone else who annoys me instead.

"Like Uncle Kevin," he adds.
Which makes me laugh.

But Mom is giving the EVIL EYE now.
(Uh-oh!)

When we get home, Dad and I escape to his shed to eat his secret stash of caramel wafers. (TREAT!)

It's the last day of the term tomorrow. So I MUSTN'T FORGET.

I only have tonight to finish my review homework. (It's the last thing I have left to do.)

I know, I'll review the school concert. That won't take long!
Just eat the last wafer biscuit and wrap it up for Delia first.... Ha, ha!
And draw a few more pictures.

THEN I'll start my homework....

.......in the morning.

(I'll have LOADS of time
to do it if I get up early tomorrow.)

This is a good idea.

Mr. Fullerman, I'm **SO** sorry about my REVIEW homework.

As you can see I DID do it.

Let me explain.

I was on my way to school when I was followed and

AttACKED

by a **VICIOUS** dog.

I defended myself with the only thing I could think of.

My notebook.

LUCKILY I survived (just).

But my REVIEW HOMEWORK didn't....

Sorry again....

Oh dear, Tom.
I was looking forward to finally
reading it.
You will just have do it again over
the break.
In the meantime, let's hope you don't
get abducted by aliens
or attacked by GIANTS.
What an eventful life you have.
See you (and your homework) next
term.

Mr. Fullerman

(Result!)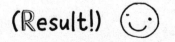

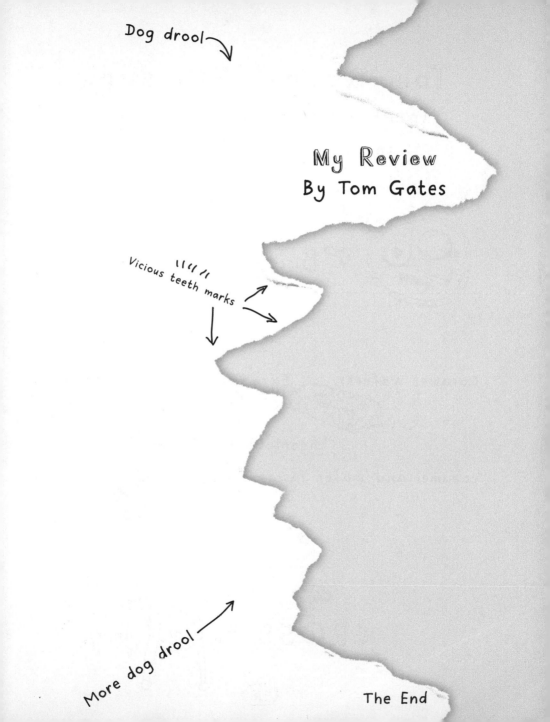

Tom Gates' Glossary

(Which means explanations for stuff
that might sound a bit ODD.)

Yum!

Biscuits = cookies.

Caramel wafers: Excellent biscuits (cookies)
covered in
chocolate with layers of
caramel and wafer inside.

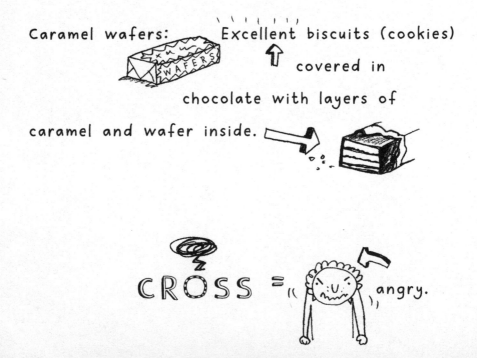

CROSS = angry.

Dodgy ≡ something that's a bit ODD or wrong. Maybe slightly peculiar or not quite right. For instance: That apple looks a bit Dodgy.

That monster looks  a bit dodgy. ←(worm)

Headmaster Mr. Keen is a principal.

JOLLY ☺ ≡ Happy! ☺ Yeah!

A Jumper  is a sweater.

Mate = FRIEND

Derek (my best mate).

MERITS are special POINTS or STARS awarded by your teacher for excellent work.

Rumbled! basically means

You're busted!

Treat - When I say My trick worked a TREAT! that means it worked REALLY well.

Turn over for
something nicer

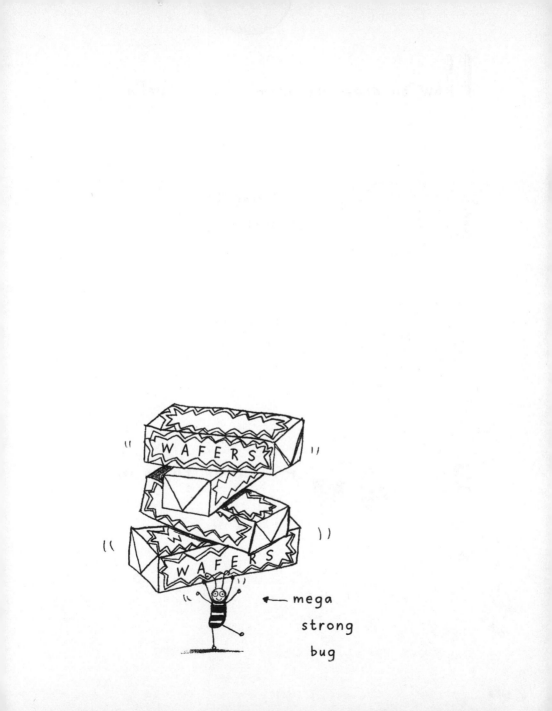

How to draw my grumpy sister Delia

1.  ← Draw this shape.

2. 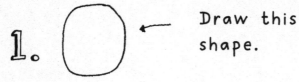 ← Then her glasses . . .

3.  ← Color them in.

4.  Ears . . . (even though
she doesn't LISTEN).

Add her
manky hair . . .

5.  . . . and add a gloom
cloud. . . .

When Liz was little, she loved to draw, paint and make things. Her mum used to say she was very good at making a mess (which is still true today!).

She kept drawing and went to art school—leaving with a BA in Graphic Design—to find her first job as a designer and art director at Jive Records U.K. She went freelance and her illustration work began to be used on a wide variety of products, which led to her first picture books and writing her own stories. Tom Gates is the first series of books Liz has written and illustrated for older children. They have won several prestigious awards, including the Roald Dahl Funny Prize, the Waterstones Children's Book Prize and the Blue Peter Book Award. The books have also been translated into over 33 languages worldwide. Liz works in a nice cozy shed in her garden and lives in (mostly) sunny Brighton with her husband and three (not so little any more) children. She doesn't have a pet but she does have lots of squirrels in the garden that eat everything in sight (including her tulip bulbs, which is annoying).

Coming soon!
Tom Gates: Excellent Excuses (and other good stuff)
Tom Gates: Everything's Amazing (Sort of)